The Birdwatchers

Simon James

CANDLEWICK PRESS

For all my friends
in upstate New York —

Jeanette and Hank,
Louis and Roseanna,
Annie and Leah,
Val,
and especially Debbie,
fellow adventurer
and custodian of my beloved
motorized scooter

First U.S. edition 2002

Library of Congress Cataloging-in-Publication Data

James, Simon, date.
The birdwatchers / Simon James. — 1st U.S. ed.
p. cm.
Summary: Intrigued by her granddad's stories of what happens
when he goes birdwatching, Jess decides to accompany him one day.
ISBN 0-7636-1676-1
[1. Bird watching — Fiction. 2. Birds — Fiction. 3. Grandfathers — Fiction.] I. Title.
PZ7.J1544 Bi 2002
[E] — dc21   2001025650

2 4 6 8 10 9 7 5 3 1

Printed in Italy

This book was typeset in Garamond ITC Book Condensed.
The illustrations were done in watercolor and ink.

Candlewick Press
2067 Massachusetts Avenue
Cambridge, Massachusetts 02140

visit us at www.candlewick.com

My granddad is a birdwatcher.

He tells me birdwatching stories.

He always says, "Jess, when I go

birdwatching, things happen."

Once my granddad said,
"Jess, when I make drawings
of the birds, sometimes they
make drawings of me, too."

My granddad said, "Jess,
sometimes the birds help me
when I can't find their names
in my bird book."

And my granddad said, "Jess,
I got all the birds together
one morning to record
something called the
dawn chorus, just for you."

My granddad said,
"Birds are amazing, Jess."
But I wasn't sure. I had
to find out for myself.

So one day I decided to go
birdwatching with him.
When we got there, I couldn't
believe it.

I couldn't see anything at all.

Granddad showed me how to use
his binoculars. Everything was
closer. But I couldn't see anything.
Nothing happened.

Then Granddad took me
to the birdwatching hut.

Granddad opened the hatch
and we looked out.
It was amazing.

I'd never seen so many birds.
Granddad said there were
Yellow Warblers, Ring-necked
Ducks, herons, snipe, and
Western Grebes. We made lots
of notes and loads of drawings.

Soon it was time to go.
On the way back Granddad
asked me what I liked best
about my first day birdwatching.

That's when I thought
I'd tell him a birdwatching
story of my own.

"Granddad, I liked it best when
the dancing penguins came
and shared my sandwich."

"Dancing penguins, Jess?"
said Granddad.
"I must have been
looking the other way."

The End